# The Abominable Snowman Doesn't Roast Marshmallows

# Want more Bailey School Kids?
# Check these out!

 #1-50

# SUPER SPECIALS #1-6

 #1-10

# And don't miss the . . .
# HOLIDAY SPECIALS

*Swamp Monsters Don't Chase Wild Turkeys*
*Aliens Don't Carve Jack-o'-lanterns*
*Mrs. Claus Doesn't Climb Telephone Poles*
*Leprechauns Don't Play Fetch*
*Ogres Don't Hunt Easter Eggs*

# The Abominable Snowman Doesn't Roast Marshmallows

by **Debbie Dadey**
**and**
**Marcia Thornton Jones**

illustrated by John Steven Gurney

A
**LITTLE APPLE**
PAPERBACK

**SCHOLASTIC INC.**
New York   Toronto   London   Auckland   Sydney
Mexico City   New Delhi   Hong Kong   Buenos Aires

ISBN 0-439-65037-2

24 23 22 21 20 19 18 17                                    14 15 16/0

Printed in the U.S.A.                                              40

First printing, January 2005

# Contents

# 1

# Blizzard

"Watch out!" Eddie yelled, but he was too late. The school bus drove by and splashed Melody, Howie, and Liza. "You guys look like kidsicles," Eddie said with a snicker.

Liza shivered as icicles formed on her nose. "It's not funny. You'd think that bus driver would watch where he's going."

"Maybe he gets extra money from the school board if he splashes kids," Eddie said with a laugh. The kids looked both ways before crossing Delaware Boulevard on their way home from school. Snow already covered the streets and sidewalks, and more continued to fall. It even covered the red freckles on Eddie's nose.

"Maybe we'll get a snow day out of this," Eddie said hopefully.

Liza shook her head. "My mother told me that it would have to be really bad before we missed any more school. We've already had too many snow days this year."

Eddie sighed and shook the bushes on the corner. Huge blobs of snow plopped to the ground.

"I'm so cold my goosebumps are trying to fly south for the winter," Melody said, rubbing the damp sleeves of her winter coat.

"Nobody was expecting this much snow," Howie said. "The weatherman on WMTJ said that weather patterns around the world have been very unusual lately. In fact," Howie continued, "the Himalayan Mountains are experiencing a strange warm spell."

Eddie stared at his friend. Howie was a smart kid who wanted to be a doctor when he grew up, but sometimes he still surprised Eddie. "How do you know those things?" Eddie asked.

Howie shrugged. "You can learn a lot from TV if you watch the right channels."

"I'm glad we aren't having a warm spell," Liza said. "The annual Winter Frost Carnival wouldn't seem right without snow."

Every year Bailey City held a Winter Carnival, complete with a parade, a snow sculpture contest, snowball fights, and human dogsled races. The carnival was just a few days away and the kids were looking forward to all of the competitions.

Melody knocked a pile of white stuff off her black pigtails. "A *little* snow would be okay, but this is ridiculous," she said.

Wet snow pelted the kids so hard they could barely see the sidewalk. "Why don't you guys come over to my house?" Howie suggested. "We could get started on our snow sculpture."

"Great idea," Eddie said. "We've got to come up with something that will beat that weird family over on Dedman Street."

His friends nodded. They knew exactly

4

who he meant. Last year a family living in a rundown house had made a haunted ice village on their front lawn. The judges took one look and gave them first prize.

"Don't worry," Eddie continued. "I've got it all planned. We'll fill Howie's yard with snow monsters!"

Liza shook her head so hard her cap slipped off her blonde hair. "I wanted to make an ice princess castle."

Eddie glared at Liza. "That's the silliest thing I've ever heard. Snow monsters are much cooler."

Melody interrupted them before they could say another word. "Maybe we should work on another contest for now," she said.

The kids stopped at the corner of Main Street and Delaware Boulevard. It was snowing so hard that the streetlight had come on.

"Holy Toledo!" Eddie shouted, totally ignoring Melody. "Look at that!"

# 2

# Great Balls of Fire

"Oh my gosh," Liza screeched. "It's a forest fire!"

In the empty lot across Main Street the kids could plainly see a roaring blaze. The red flames stood out against the white ground like a flashing electric sign.

Eddie rolled his eyes. "We're not in a forest."

"Well, it's a fire," Liza said.

Melody nodded. "We have to call for help fast before it spreads to one of our houses."

"Great balls of fire!" Eddie screamed. "Help! Help!"

Melody punched Eddie in the arm. "Not here, you dope, we have to get to a phone and call the fire department."

The kids tried to run, but it was slow

7

going in their winter boots. They only made it a few feet through the drifting snow before they were panting and their boots were filled with snow.

"Yuck," Eddie snapped. "I'm turning into Frosty the Toeman!"

"The city will burn down before we get to a phone," Liza shrieked.

"Won't the snow put it out first?" Melody wondered.

"Wait just a minute," Howie said, squinting through the falling snow. "That's no wildfire. That's a huge campfire."

"In the middle of a snowstorm?" Liza squeaked.

"In the middle of a town?" Melody asked.

"Nobody is that crazy," Eddie said.

"It looks like someone is — and there's the guy now," Howie said, pointing out the shape of a huge man hunched over the fire. Through the swirling snow, the kids spotted his very large shadow beside the roaring flames.

8

"Hey, I think you're right," Eddie said. "That *is* a guy. A very big guy."

"Every person with half a brain is staying inside on a day like this," Melody said. The wind changed directions and blew directly into her face. She sputtered to catch her breath.

"Maybe the poor guy doesn't have a home to go to," Liza said over the blowing wind.

"He's got to be a nutcase," Melody said, shaking her head. This time the wind blew so hard she fell onto her rear end.

Eddie laughed. "Maybe you're the nutcase. Let's go see this man."

"No!" Liza squealed. Eddie didn't like to listen to anyone but himself. He headed across the street, right for the mysterious stranger.

# 3

## Savage

"Hi! My name is Eddie and these are my friends, Melody and Howie. Liza is the girl hiding behind Melody."

"How do you do?" Liza asked in a very small voice.

The giant man didn't even glance up at the four kids. Hunched over the fire, he looked like a cross between a polar bear and an ape. He wore a furry white coat, hat, and gloves. Even his boots were made of thick white fur. Shaggy blond hair peeked out from beneath his hat and a fine layer of frost covered the beard on his face. In places, the frost had melted from the heat of the fire and water dribbled down his face. He held a stick over the flames. On the tip of the stick sat three plump marshmallows.

"What's your name?" Eddie asked.

The man slowly turned his head. He stared at the four kids long enough for snowflakes to cling to his eyelashes. "Savage," he said finally. "Call me Savage." His words were muddled by a thick accent, and his voice was as deep as a tuba.

"You want?" he asked. The man held out the stick, now covered in honey-colored roasted marshmallows.

"Awesome," Eddie said, reaching out for one. Liza pulled Eddie's hand away. "Sorry, Mr. Savage," she said, "we can't take anything from strangers."

The man shrugged his huge fur-covered shoulders and popped the three marshmallows into his mouth. As soon as he had finished chewing, he turned back to the fire as if the kids were nothing more than bothersome fleas. He jabbed more marshmallows on the stick and held them over the fire.

"I don't think talking to Mr. Savage is

such a good idea," Liza whispered in Melody's ear. "What if he's a cat burglar or a bank robber? What if he's an ax murderer?"

"Even if he isn't," Melody whispered back, "he's still a stranger and we should leave him alone."

Eddie, on the other hand, couldn't hear their whispers. He kicked through the snow to get even closer to Mr. Savage. "That's a big fire," Eddie said. "It sure looks warm. I didn't think we were allowed to build fires in the middle of town."

"Kids," the man grunted and slowly shook his shaggy head, "should never build fires."

Eddie grinned. "I bet I could build a fire. A big fire. A fire big enough to melt all the snow in Bailey City!"

The man turned so fast that a shower of snow from his enormous shoulders sprayed Eddie. "No!" Mr. Savage growled. "No fire for kids."

"Yikes," Liza whimpered. "We'd better

get out of here before he stomps Eddie into slush."

Howie nodded and grabbed Eddie's sleeve just as the huge man rose to his feet. Mr. Savage stood as tall as a nearby tree, and as massive as a boulder. Melody couldn't take her eyes off the gigantic stranger.

Howie could. He looked around for a quick escape. When he did, he couldn't believe what he saw.

# 4

## Squash

A pickup truck with a flatbed trailer was parked nearby under a drooping spruce tree. Nestled in the corner of the vacant lot beyond the tree, Mr. Savage had built a snow house that looked like an igloo. In front of the igloo were snow chairs, a snow table, and what even looked like a snow bed.

Mr. Savage reached out, causing Melody and Liza to jump back, but he ignored the kids and grabbed a huge bag of marshmallows.

"Hey," Eddie said. "Those are Mega-Marshmallows. They're the best marshmallows ever!" If there was one thing Eddie was an expert on, it was sweets.

The man grunted as he sat down again. He plucked three more marshmallows

from the bag and jabbed them onto the end of his stick.

"Do you live here?" Howie asked, forgetting all about leaving. He was just too curious. Besides, Mr. Savage didn't look nearly as scary when he wasn't standing.

"I travel. Do jobs," Mr. Savage said, turning the stick so the marshmallows roasted an even brown. "Look for cousin," he said.

"Does your cousin live near Bailey City?" Melody asked politely.

Mr. Savage nodded his shaggy head. "He sent postcard. From here. So I visit. Maybe live here, too."

"Live here?" Liza said with a shaky voice.

Mr. Savage slowly pulled the three marshmallows from the stick and plopped them in his mouth all at once. While he chewed, he jammed on three more marshmallows and held them over the flames. When he finally swallowed, Mr. Savage turned to look Liza straight in the eyes.

"Cousin said nice mountain here," Mr. Savage told her. "Good food. Fresh meat."

Eddie didn't care about Mr. Savage's cousin. Eddie wanted one of those marshmallows, and he wanted it bad. "You should let the marshmallows catch on fire," Eddie suggested. "Then you can watch them burn. When you blow them out, they're black. I like them when they're crunchy like that."

Mr. Savage grunted and Liza started to feel less scared. In fact, she felt a bit sorry for him. It was cold, the snow was falling even faster, and all he had for dinner was roasted marshmallows. A cold wind whistled through the spruce tree's branches and made her shiver. Maybe the man needed a warm place to spend the night.

"You know," Liza said softly, "my church is just down the street. They have a warm bed there you could sleep in. You could get in out of the snow."

For the first time, Mr. Savage smiled.

His huge pointed teeth gleamed in the firelight and his eyes glowed red. "Snow! Me like snow!"

"Okay, then maybe we could help you find your cousin," Melody suggested. "You could stay with him. What's his name?"

The man slowly looked from kid to kid. "Squash," he finally said. "His name Squash."

Then he roared so loudly, Melody couldn't help screaming, "Run!"

# 5

## Nutcase

The kids didn't stop running until they were inside Howie's house with the door locked. "Why did you run?" Eddie asked, once he caught his breath. "I didn't even get a single roasted marshmallow."

"That guy was scary," Melody admitted. She took off her wet boots and left them by the door in Howie's kitchen.

Howie grabbed packets of hot chocolate from a cabinet and turned on the hot water faucet. "It seems like he's really living outside."

Liza grabbed a mug and looked out the kitchen window. "I hope he'll be okay. What if he freezes to death out there?"

Eddie ripped open a packet of hot chocolate. Brown powder exploded all over the counter. Eddie scooped some into his hand and sniffed before licking his hand clean. "Only some kind of nutty snowman would want to sleep outside in this weather."

Melody nodded. "You're right. We never should have gone near him, but not because he's crazy."

"You're crazy and we hang around you," Eddie said before licking the rest of the chocolate powder off the counter.

Melody gave Eddie a warning look. Howie stepped between them, handing Melody a cup of steaming hot chocolate from the microwave. "If it's not because he's crazy, then why?" Howie asked.

"Didn't you hear what he said?" Melody asked. "He's looking for his cousin." She blew on her hot chocolate and stared at her friends with big brown eyes.

"Who cares?" Eddie said. "My grandmother makes me visit my cousins every summer. It's boring, but not against the law."

"Eddie has a point. Lots of people visit

relatives," Liza agreed. She sat down at the kitchen table and stirred her hot chocolate.

When Howie brought out a bag of marshmallows, Eddie grabbed a handful and plopped them into his mug. His cup overflowed with chocolate drink and white foam. Then he stuffed his mouth with more marshmallows. "These Mega-Marshmallows are the best," Eddie said as white chunks dribbled out of the corners of his mouth.

Melody shook her head at Eddie. "I guess more than one monster around here likes marshmallows."

"What are you talking about?" Howie asked. "What monster?"

Eddie stuffed even more marshmallows into his mouth until he looked like a crazy chipmunk. "Eddie, of course," Melody said. "But I'm also talking about Mr. Savage."

"What?" Howie and Eddie said together. Only Eddie's mouth was so full, it sounded more like, *"Blat?"* And when

Eddie opened his mouth, he accidentally spit marshmallows all over the kitchen counter.

Liza ducked to avoid getting hit by flying marshmallow chunks. Melody picked a bit of marshmallow off her shoulder and wrinkled her nose. "Mr. Savage said his cousin's name was Squash," Melody told her friends.

Liza gasped. "That's right! Don't you guys remember meeting Mr. Squash?"

Eddie looked at Howie and shrugged. Both boys had blank looks on their faces. "Is he the guy who stocks the vegetables at Turner's Market? The one with the green hair?" Eddie asked.

Melody shook her head and glared at Eddie. "I can't believe you don't remember."

Liza's face turned pale. "Square dancing," she blurted out. "Mr. Squash taught us square dancing on our school trip to Ruby Mountain."

Eddie spit out the hot chocolate he had just sipped as he suddenly remembered Mr. Squash. "Thanks a lot," Eddie said. "I've tried to forget all about square dancing." Everyone knew that the last thing Eddie liked was dancing.

Mr. Squash, their square-dance teacher, had been so tall his head had nearly touched the ceiling of the picnic shelter. He had a long beard and the hair on his head curled over his collar. But the strangest thing about him was a pair of feet big enough to stomp a tree into splinters. The kids had all been convinced that he was the legendary Bigfoot.

"Wait a minute," Howie said, holding up his hand to stop his friends from talking. "We never proved that Mr. Squash was Bigfoot."

"We never proved he wasn't, either," Melody said, "and now Mr. Savage is saying they're cousins."

"And if Mr. Savage is Bigfoot's cousin," Liza said with a shaky voice, "that can only mean one thing."

"Mr. Savage," Melody said with a nod, "is the Abominable Snowman!"

# 6

# Winter Carnival

Eddie laughed so hard, more marshmallows went flying across the room. Even Howie smiled.

"Your brains must've turned to Mega-Marshmallow fluff," Eddie said. "The Abominable Snowman doesn't roast marshmallows!"

Liza didn't laugh. Neither did Melody. "This is serious," Melody said, but Eddie didn't listen.

He gulped down the rest of his hot chocolate and wiped his mouth with the back of his hand. "I've had enough talk about big crazy guys," Eddie said.

"We should get ready for the Winter Frost Carnival," Howie agreed.

Eddie rubbed his hands together. "Now you're talking. Let's get started building

snow monsters for the ice sculpture contest!"

"No!" Liza snapped. "We're making an ice princess castle."

"We could enter the human dogsled race instead of the ice sculpture contest," Melody said, to stop Liza and Eddie from arguing. "They have an elementary division this year. I bet we could win first place if we practiced."

Liza's eyes lit up. "First prize is a free ski weekend at the Golden Egg Ski Lodge."

The kids threw their soggy coats, boots, hats, and gloves back on. "We'll use my old sled," Howie said. He grabbed some rope from his garage and hooked it up to the front of his orange sled.

Eddie put his back to the wind and told his friends, "Liza is the lightest, so she should sit on the sled and everyone else can pull her."

"Works for me," Liza said, hopping in Howie's sled.

"I'm the strongest so I'll be in front," Eddie said.

"You're not any stronger than me," Melody snapped.

Howie held up his snow-covered gloves. "It doesn't matter who's first, we're just practicing."

"All right, let's go, team!" Eddie said from the front of the line. Melody, Howie, and Eddie pulled, but nothing happened.

"What have you been eating lately, Liza?" Melody asked. "Bricks?"

"Let's try it again," Howie suggested. "This time, pull together on three. One, two, three!" The three kids pulled as hard as they could. The runners dug into the deep snow. The sled creaked and shuddered, but very slowly it started to move. At first just by inches, then by a foot, the sled began to glide more easily through the snow.

"You're doing it!" Liza screamed. "Keep it up!"

It was tough going for Melody, Howie, and Eddie in their winter boots, but they finally managed to get Liza moving pretty fast.

"Don't go out in the street," Howie yelled when they got to the end of his yard. Eddie turned quickly, and so did Melody and Howie. Unfortunately the sled didn't.

Liza and the sled flew into a huge snowdrift at the end of Howie's drive-

way. Only the back of the sled and Liza's boots stuck out of the snow.

Eddie laughed, but Melody pulled Liza out of the drift. "Are you okay?" Melody asked. "You look like the Abominable Snowman."

"She looks more like something from the frozen food section of the grocery store to me," Eddie teased.

Liza sat on the ground for a few minutes, feeling like a petrified monster. She shivered and knocked snow off her neck. "Oh, no," she exclaimed. "I just remembered that Mr. Savage said Bailey City was full of food, including fresh meat. You don't really think he was talking about us, do you?"

Melody gasped. "You're right! What else would a snow monster mean?"

"Wait a minute," Howie said. "Even if Mr. Savage is the Abominable Snowman, he wouldn't stay in Bailey City for long because there isn't enough snow."

"Are you sure?" Melody asked, looking

around their neighborhood. Snowdrifts covered every yard and even more snow was falling. In the distance, Ruby Mountain stood tall and white against the gray sky. "I think the Abominable Snowman has moved to Bailey City — and he's brought winter with him!"

"That can't be right," Howie gasped.

"A little snow doesn't mean anything," Eddie added.

"Then I guess we'll have to prove it," Melody said. "Before Bailey City becomes the winter feeding ground of the Abominable Snowman!"

# 7

# Feeding Ground

The next morning, Liza's telephone rang. It was Melody. "You have to get over here," Melody whispered through the phone.

"But we'll be late for school," Liza warned her friend.

"Being late for school is the least of our worries," Melody told her before hanging up the phone and calling Howie.

"But I'm rewriting the opening paragraph of my science paper," Howie told her.

"Forget science," Melody told Howie. "We have a problem bigger than science. Way bigger."

When Melody called Eddie, he was eating breakfast. "I haven't had my cereal yet," he complained. "I can't go out without my Wheaties."

"Even they won't make you strong enough to deal with this problem," Melody warned him. "Now hurry!"

Liza, Howie, and Eddie made it to Melody's at the same time. She waited for them under the streetlight in front of her house. It was so early that the light still shone brightly on the falling snow.

Snow already covered Melody's pigtails. She held her finger to her mouth to keep her friends from talking. She led them around a drift and kicked through snow until they were in her backyard.

"What's this about?" Howie asked.

"My boots are full of snow," Liza complained.

"I'm hungry," Eddie added.

"You won't care when you see what I found," Melody told them. She pointed to the ground outside her bedroom window.

Howie, Liza, and Eddie looked where she pointed. Then they looked at Melody. "You made me miss breakfast to show me snow?" Eddie sputtered.

Melody rolled her eyes. "You're not really looking!" she told them.

Her friends looked again, this time more closely. "It can't be!" Liza finally said.

"We must be imagining it," Howie said. He rubbed his eyes and looked again.

"They're real," Melody said with a nod as she moved closer to the giant footprints that covered her backyard. The falling snow was rapidly filling up the footprints.

Eddie stepped in one of the tracks. He could fit both his boots in one, with room to spare. "These don't look like they were made by a boot," he said. "They look like they were made by a bare foot. A *giant* bare foot."

"Whoever made those tracks is huge," Liza said.

"Whoever made them should not be wandering around in their bare feet. They could get frostbitten," Howie added. Since Howie planned on being a doctor, he always worried about people's health.

Melody shook her head. "Whatever made those tracks doesn't have to worry about the cold," she said.

"You mean you know who made them?" Howie asked.

"Of course I do," Melody said.

"Who?" Liza asked.

"Not who," Melody said. "*What*. It was the Abominable Snowman!"

Eddie flopped onto a mound of snow. "Nobody believes in that monster snowman fairy tale," he said.

"Besides," Howie added. "Even if the

Abominable Snowman was real *and* was visiting Bailey City, why would he be tromping around your yard?"

"That's easy," Melody said seriously. "He was looking for dinner."

Liza gulped. Howie gasped. Not Eddie. He laughed. "Well, if the Abominable Snowman likes brains, he's not going to find any around your house."

Melody waited for Eddie to stop laughing. Then she looked him square in the eyes. "What makes you think he was only in *my* yard?" she asked.

Liza's mouth flew open. She squeaked, but no words came out. She didn't need to talk, though. Melody knew exactly what Liza was thinking. "If I'm right," Melody said, "your yards will be full of tracks, too."

The kids looked at Melody like she was crazy, but only for a moment. Then they were off, running as fast as they could in their snow boots. First they went to Liza's house. Then they stopped by Howie's. Finally they raced to Eddie's backyard. Sure enough, at each place it was the same. Tracks, so big and deep that even the falling snow couldn't hide them, covered every yard.

"Do you really think the Abominable Snowman was in our yards last night?" Liza asked in a hushed whisper.

Melody nodded. "And if I'm right, I know exactly where these tracks will lead us. Right back to Mr. Savage's snowy campsite!"

# 8

## Super Spy

"We don't have time for monster tracking," Howie said. "We have to get to school."

"And I have to get some food," Eddie added.

"Besides," Howie said slowly, "I'm sure there's a logical explanation for these tracks, because there's no such thing as the Abominable Snowman."

"Oh, yeah?" Melody challenged. "Then tell me. What's the logical explanation?"

Howie blinked. He scratched the hair under his cap. Finally he shook his head. "I don't know. Let me think on it."

Liza patted Melody on her shoulder as Howie and Eddie headed inside Eddie's kitchen for a quick bowl of cereal. "Maybe the boys are right," Liza said. "Let's forget about this monster story."

But Liza might as well have told Melody to show up at school in just her underwear. Either way, it wasn't going to happen. There was no way Melody could forget those monster tracks outside her house.

That afternoon, Melody was very quiet as the four friends left school and headed for Bailey City Park, where the floats were being built. A giant parade kicked off the Winter Frost Carnival and the kids always went to the park for a sneak preview.

There was one float carved out of white foam that looked like a village in the North Pole. It was made by the workers at the electric company. Another float didn't look wintry at all. It had palm trees with a hammock tied between them. The sign on the side of the float said BAILEY CITY TRAVEL AGENCY. Liza pulled her friends to-

ward a float that included a castle painted
white and covered with glitter. "See?" she
said. "I told you an ice princess castle
would be perfect for our ice sculpture."

"But the librarians from the Bailey City
library already used your idea," Howie
said. "So if we build an ice sculpture, we'll
have to think of something else."

"I already thought of something else," Eddie argued. "Monsters."

The four friends made their way from one float to another. Suddenly, Melody grabbed them and pointed down at the ground. Amidst the tracks made by dogs' paws and kids' boots were bare-feet tracks. And not just any feet. Huge feet.

"He's here," Melody whispered. "The Abominable Snowman is here."

"Does that mean your imaginary monster likes parades?" Eddie asked in an innocent voice.

Melody ignored his teasing. "If the Abominable Snowman is spying on the parade, it can mean only one thing. There is something here he wants."

"Like what?" Howie asked.

"Think about it," Melody said. "Every year, the entire town of Bailey City lines the streets to watch the parade that kicks off the carnival. We're all in one place at the same time. That makes it a perfect time for the Abominable Snowman to attack! If we don't do something fast, the parade will be a disaster and the carnival will be ruined. But worse than that, the entire town will be in danger."

Eddie laughed. "Since there *is* no Abominable Snowman, there is absolutely nothing to worry about."

"If you're that sure, then you won't

mind doing a little spying on Mr. Savage after school tomorrow, will you?" Melody asked.

Eddie grinned and patted Melody on the back. "Of course not," he said. "After all, Super Spy is my middle name!"

# 9

# Horror Movie

"Let's do it!" Melody said as soon as the school bell rang the next afternoon.

"Are you sure this is a good idea?" Liza asked her friends as they headed down the hallway outside their third grade classroom. "What if Mr. Savage really *is* the Abominable Snowman?"

"His name sounds more like a professional wrestler to me," Eddie said with a snicker. He opened the outside door and a blast of whirling snow hit him in the face.

"I'd rather read a book and sip hot chocolate," Howie admitted, "but at least Mr. Savage's campsite is on our way home."

The four kids pulled their hats down

and their scarves up until only their eyes showed. They looked like mummies stomping down Delaware Boulevard.

"Do you see anything?" Liza asked when they got to Main Street.

"I don't think he's there," Howie said.

Liza gulped as they crossed the street. "Maybe he's waiting to pounce on us, like in those horror movies."

"How many horror movies have you ever seen?" Eddie asked Liza. He knew she didn't like anything scary, and that her mother wouldn't let her watch anything that wasn't rated G.

"Well, only part of one," Liza admitted. "I saw it at my cousin's house and it gave me nightmares for weeks."

"This isn't a movie," Melody told her friends, "this is real life. So be careful — and be ready to run."

Liza whimpered, but she followed her friends. The snow fell harder and it was already growing darker. She didn't want to go across Main Street, but she definitely didn't want to walk home alone, either.

The kids trudged as quietly as possible in their snow boots. They searched around the fire pit and the snow house. Eddie sat on the snow chair. "Hey, this isn't bad. It doesn't even feel like snow."

"I'm not sure what I expected to find," Melody said, "but there's nothing here."

"What about this?" Howie asked. He plucked a travel brochure for a ski resort in Colorado from a snowdrift.

"Winter Park," Liza read. "The perfect place for cold weather fun."

"Speaking of cold weather," Eddie complained, "I'm freezing and starving. Let's go get a snack at my house. Maybe Grandma will let us roast marshmallows over the gas stove."

But Melody wasn't ready to leave yet. "Wait," she said. "I bet I know where to find Mr. Savage."

"He's probably at Fred Barbo's Sportarama buying long underwear," Eddie snapped.

"Nope," Melody told her friends. "He's on Ruby Mountain looking for his cousin. We have to save Bailey City before a monster reunion crashes our parade."

"Bailey City doesn't need saving,"Eddie said. "But if we go to Ruby Mountain, I could try out my new sled."

Liza shook her head. "No way. I'm not sledding on Ruby Mountain. It's too dangerous."

"Not as dangerous as the Abominable Snowman using Bailey City for his hunting ground," Melody pointed out.

"Well," Liza said, "we can't go now, because it's already getting dark."

Melody nodded. "You're right. That means we'll have to go first thing in the morning. Tomorrow is Saturday, so we don't have to worry about school."

"But the parade is tomorrow!" Howie

said. "And we can't miss the human dogsled race."

"Set your alarms for six o'clock," Melody said. "And meet at my house. It's our last chance to save Bailey City from a snow monster attack!"

# 10

## Yeti

*Shriiiiiiieeeeeekkkkkkk!*

"Did you hear that?" Liza squealed.

The four kids stopped dead in their snowy tracks on Ruby Mountain. It was the next morning and a strange sound filled the frosty air. The kids were bundled against the cold, and Eddie pulled his new Z-model sled behind him. They had been trudging through the snow for what seemed like hours already.

*Shriiiiieeeeeekkkkk!*

"There it goes again," Melody said with a gulp.

"It sounds like someone scratching their fingernails on a huge chalkboard," Eddie said, looking around at the snow-covered trees.

"There are no chalkboards on Ruby

Mountain," Melody told her friends. "But there *is* a snow monster. Look!"

Melody pointed to a huge set of footprints leading up the mountain. They were big and humanlike, and whoever or whatever made the prints hadn't been wearing shoes. "We have to follow them," she said.

"But the parade will be starting soon, and my ears are cold," Liza said. "We've run out of time. We have to go back."

"We can't go back now," Melody said. "We have to find out what Mr. Savage is up to. Bailey City depends on us!" With that, Melody turned and trudged through the snow, following the line of giant tracks.

"I think I know what made that sound. And if I'm right, then Melody was right, too," Howie said as they all followed Melody. "Yeti monsters are known to communicate with whistling sounds."

"Yeti?" Eddie asked. "Is that some kind of yellow spaghetti?"

Howie shook his head. "*Yeti* is another name for the Abominable Snowman."

"There he is!" Liza screamed when the kids walked into a clearing.

Mr. Savage stood on skis at the top of a treeless slope. Far below, at the base of Ruby Mountain, sat Bailey City. Even from their high perch on the mountain, the kids could see the rest of the town lining the sidewalks, and several floats moving down Main Street.

Mr. Savage's skis were pointed straight toward town. When he saw the kids, he threw back his head. His roar echoed across the mountainside.

"Stop!" Melody ordered, as she hurried to jump in his path.

Mr. Savage roared again. "No time!" he yelled. "Out of my way!" Mr. Savage pushed off. He skied past Melody, spraying her with snow.

"Stop him!" Melody yelled. Howie and Eddie lobbed snowballs, but they just splatted against Mr. Savage's broad back and fell to the ground.

"He's getting away!" Melody moaned.

"Jump on!" Eddie told his friends. They all piled onto Eddie's sled and took off down the slopes. Trees blurred past. They flew up and over small hills, all the while keeping Mr. Savage in sight.

"Ahhhhh!" Liza screamed and closed her eyes.

"He's heading straight for the parade!" Howie shouted.

"Faster!" Melody screamed as they zipped along. "It's up to us to stop him!"

# 11

# Crash Landing

Eddie leaned forward and the sled flew past bushes and trees. Snow scattered behind them and Liza screamed as they reached the bottom of Ruby Mountain. In front of them, Mr. Savage pushed his ski poles into the snow and careened toward the last in a long line of floats.

"Can't you make this thing go faster?" Melody screamed.

"We ran out of mountain," Eddie yelled over his shoulder. "We're slowing down."

"Quick," Howie said as he jumped off. "Pull!"

Melody, Howie, and Eddie jumped off the sled and grabbed the rope before Liza could move. She gripped the sides of the sled as her three friends pulled her down the side of Main Street. The sidewalks and roads had been cleared, but new snow created a thin layer that glistened with ice. The sled moved faster and faster.

Just ahead of them, Mr. Savage had reached the last float. With a roar, he skied onto a ramp and soared through the air, landing on top of the manmade snow scene.

"We're going to be too late," Melody cried. "We have to stop him! There's no telling what he'll do."

Melody, Eddie, and Howie pumped their legs even harder. Their ragged breath left white clouds hanging in the air, and snow from their boots flew up in Liza's face. They pulled Liza and the sled past a cluster of judges. They veered around a few other kids who seemed to be standing still on their own sleds. They even zoomed past a grandstand where the mayor stood. Everything was a blur to Liza.

"We're going too fast," Liza screamed. "Stop!"

The Z-model sled was meant to go fast,

but even the Z-model wasn't supposed to go *this* fast. There was no way Eddie, Melody, and Howie could control it, especially when they hit a patch of ice. Melody slipped. Howie skidded. They both tumbled into Eddie. They all landed right in Liza's lap, but Eddie's super-duper Z-model sled didn't stop. It hit the ice and went even faster.

"AAAAAAHHHHHHHHH!" Liza screamed as the sled hit a bump and went airborne. For what seemed like an eternity, the sled sailed through the air. The four kids held on for dear life. Then the sled crash-landed right onto the float next to Mr. Savage.

The final float featured a snow scene complete with a snow hut, snow chair, and even a snow bed. Eddie, Melody, Liza, and Howie landed right in the middle of it. That's when they found out the hut wasn't made of snow at all.

# 12

## MegaFloat

The float was made out of marshmallows! MegaMarshmallows, to be exact.

Marshmallows smashed onto the kids' snowsuits. They tangled in their hair. They stuck to their noses. Marshmallows flew through the air. The crowd lining the street grabbed at the sugar fluffs and cheered.

Then the kids heard something that turned their blood to ice. Mr. Savage stood at the front of the float and held his head. "Float!" he howled. "You ruined my float!"

"Your float?" Melody asked.

Mr. Savage nodded without lifting his head from his hands. "It's my job," he moaned. "I travel. Work for MegaMarshmallow Company. But now the MegaFloat is ruined. RUINED!"

Howie, Eddie, and Liza all stared at

Melody. Melody swallowed. "I'm s . . . s . . . sorry," she stammered. "We didn't know."

"Maybe we can help put it back together," Liza said as she plucked a marshmallow from the tip of her ear and tried to stick it on the frame of the snow chair. But the kids didn't have a chance to help because just then, the mayor of Bailey City spoke over the loudspeaker.

"What a race that was!" the mayor beamed. "That can't even compare to the snow sculptures on Dedman Street! The human dogsled race is a roaring success. The winners of this year's Winter Frost Carnival race are the four kids on the MegaMarshmallow float!"

The crowd clapped. They cheered. They stomped their boots in the snow. Then they surrounded the float. They lifted Melody, Howie, Liza, Eddie, and his sled down and pushed them toward the grandstand.

"Wait," Melody said. "We have to find out if Mr. Savage found his cousin. We may not be out of danger!"

70

But Melody's words were lost in the roar of the crowd. The mayor placed a ribbon with a huge silver snowflake over each of their heads. By the time the crowd had dwindled away and the mayor had left the grandstand, Mr. Savage and his float were gone.

The next afternoon, the four kids stood in front of the empty lot on Main Street. The only sign that Mr. Savage had been there was a circle where his campfire had burned.

Eddie pulled one of Melody's pigtails. "This wintry mystery is closed," he said. "You jumped to conclusions. There was no proof Mr. Savage was the Abominable Snowman. In fact, there is no such thing as an Abominable anything!" he told her.

"I feel really bad about wrecking Mr. Savage's float," Melody admitted. "I hope he didn't lose his job."

Howie shook his head and pulled a newspaper out of his backpack. "Haven't

you guys seen the headlines? I bet he'll get a raise after our parade."

The four kids looked at the front page of the Bailey City newspaper. It showed a huge picture of the kids on the float with Mr. Savage. The caption underneath the picture read:

MEGAMARSHMALLOW FLOAT WINS!
The last float in the Winter Frost parade is a *smash* hit! Four local elementary students land in a bed of marshmallows and cause every store in town to sell out of the great-tasting treats.

"So we didn't ruin the parade after all," Melody said.

"And we did get Mr. Savage to leave," Liza told her friends.

"But the snow stopped," Eddie grumbled. "A few more inches and we could have had a snow day! I could use some more adventure."

Howie laughed. "Don't worry," he said. "Just stick around Bailey City. There's sure to be another adventure very soon!"

**Debbie Dadey and Marcia Thornton Jones** have fun writing stories together. When they both worked at an elementary school in Lexington, Kentucky, Debbie was the school librarian and Marcia was a teacher. During their lunch break in the school cafeteria, they came up with the idea of the Bailey School Kids.

Debbie and her family now live in Fort Collins, Colorado. Marcia and her husband still live in Kentucky, where she continues to teach. How do these authors write together? They talk on the phone and use computers and fax machines!

Learn more about Debbie and Marcia at their Web site, www.baileykids.com!

# Like The Bailey School Kids?

## Check out

# Ghostville Elementary®

**another spooky series by
Marcia Thornton Jones and Debbie Dadey!**

# Ghostville Elementary®
# #1 Ghost Class

The basement of Sleepy Hollow's elementary school is haunted. At least that's what everyone says. But no one has ever gone downstairs to prove it. Until now . . .

This year, Cassidy and Jeff's classroom is in the basement. But the kids aren't scared. There's no such thing as ghosts, right?

Tell that to the ghosts.

The basement belongs to another class — a *ghost* class. They don't want to share. And they will haunt Cassidy and her friends until they get their room back!

# Ghostville Elementary®
# #2 Ghost Game

It's BORING in the basement! And the ghosts in the class want to come out and play . . . with the whole school.

Watch out, Sleepy Hollow — it's haunting time!

The ghosts will only stop their horrible haunt if Jeff, Cassidy, and Nina beat them in a game of basketball. But these ghosts play to win. And they don't play by the rules.

# Ghostville Elementary®
# #3 New Ghoul in School

The new kid in Nina, Jeff, and Cassidy's class is strange! He's see-through. He floats above his chair. And he never seems to leave the classroom.

Could the new boy be a new *ghost*?

Nina and her friends are afraid to find out. And so are the other ghosts! Will this mean more fun for the class in the basement — or more haunting?

# Ghostville Elementary®
# #4 Happy Haunting!

Welcome to fright night! Mr. Morton's third graders have invited family and friends to visit their classroom. Cassidy, Jeff, and Nina are all set to turn the school basement into a haunted house for their guests. The problem is . . . the basement is already haunted! And these ghosts don't like visitors!

Can Cassidy and her classmates stop the ghosts from crashing the party? Or will their parents find out that the school is haunted . . . *for real*?

# Ghostville Elementary®
# #5 Stage Fright

It's showtime! Jeff, Cassidy, and Nina find some great props for their class play when they visit a sale at the old Blackburn Mansion. But they bring back more to their room than just an antique fiddle and pet dish. They bring more ghosts! Now the new ghosts are trying to steal the spotlight and ruin the class play. The show must go on . . . but it can't go on like this!

# Ghostville Elementary®
# #6 Happy Boo-Day to You!

It's Nina's birthday and she's going to have the best birthday party ever. But someone or some*thing* is trying to scare Nina and her party guests. Did one of the classroom ghosts follow her home? Or is Nina's birthday party being haunted by something much scarier than a Ghostville ghost?

Nina and her friends can't be sure. But they know one thing: It's time to bust these birthday bashers . . . once and for all!

# Ghostville Elementary®
# #7 Hide-and-Spook

Cassidy feels left out. She can't run or kick or swing a bat nearly as well as her friends, Jeff and Nina. Field Day is going to be a nightmare! And to make matters worse, Cassidy finds a creepy old doll in the school basement. She tries to hide it away, but it keeps coming back to haunt her. Even the classroom ghosts are scared *boo*-less!

That's when Cassidy realizes that even though she can't catch a ball, she *is* really good at something . . . finding out ghostly secrets! Ready or not, here she comes!

Ready for more spooky fun?
Then take a sneak peek
at the next

# Ghostville Elementary®

## #8 Ghosts Be Gone!

As the kids lined up at the door to go home that afternoon, they couldn't stop talking about Miss Bogart. Most of the kids still didn't believe in ghosts or ghost-hunting. Of course, Nina, Jeff, and Cassidy did. They knew ghosts were real and they knew there were ghosts in their classroom, but they didn't say a word.

"Being a ghost hunter is an awesome idea," Andrew said as Mr. Morton led the kids up the steps. A breeze swept through the leaves of nearby trees, making a whispering sound.

"Ghost-hunting would be much more exciting than counting money for a bank or writing stories for the newspaper," Andrew added.

"Maybe you could write ghost stories for the newspaper instead," Carla said.

"No way I'm going to sit at a desk and type stories into a computer," Andrew told her. "I'm going to sleep all day and spend my nights in haunted houses and cemeteries hunting ghosts."

"You don't honestly believe Miss Bogart," Darla asked, "do you?"

Andrew grinned so big the freckles on his cheeks squished together. "Not only do I believe her," he said, "but I'm going to become the youngest and bestest ghost hunter the town of Sleepy Hollow has ever seen."